KAREN LYNN WILLIAMS

GALIMOTO

ILLUSTRATED BY
CATHERINE STOCK

LOTHROP, LEE & SHEPARD BOOKS
NEW YORK

Galimoto means "car" in Chichewa, the national language of Malawi, Africa. It is also the name for a type of push toy made by children. Old wires—or sticks, cornstalks, and pieces of yam—are shaped into cars, trucks, bicycles, trains, and helicopters. All of these intricate toys are known as *galimoto* (GAL-lee-moe-toe).

The word may have come from the English *motor car*, with the words in reverse order. In Chichewa the sounds r and l are often interchanged (and c and g may have been), and every syllable ends with a vowel.

Text copyright © 1990 by Karen Lynn Williams
Illustrations copyright © 1990 by Catherine Stock

First Edition 1 2 3 4 5 6 7 8 9 10

Library of Congress Cataloging in Publication Data
Williams, Karen Lynn. Galimoto / by Karen Lynn Williams; illustrated by Catherine Stock.
p.   cm. Summary: Walking through his village, a young African boy finds the materials to make a special toy.
ISBN 0-688-08789-2.—ISBN 0-688-08790-6 (lib. bdg.)   [1. Toy making—Fiction.   2. Africa—Fiction.]   I. Stock, Catherine, ill.   II. Title   PZ7.W66655Gal   1990   [E]—dc19   89-2258 CIP AC

For my mother, who knows about children,
and for the children of Nsanje, who know
about galimotos

K.L.W.

For Val and John and Megan and Vanessa and the Robinsons

C.S.

Kondi opened an old shoe box and looked inside. These were his things. They belonged to him. Inside the box there was a ball made of many old plastic bags, tightly wrapped with string. There was a knife Kondi had made from a piece of tin can and a dancing man he had made from dried cornstalks. In Kondi's box there were also some scraps of wire. He had been saving the wires for something special. Now he took them and the knife from his box.

"I shall make a galimoto," Kondi told his
brother, Ufulu.

Ufulu laughed. "A boy with only seven years
cannot make such a toy. You don't have enough
wire."

"I will get enough wire," Kondi answered.

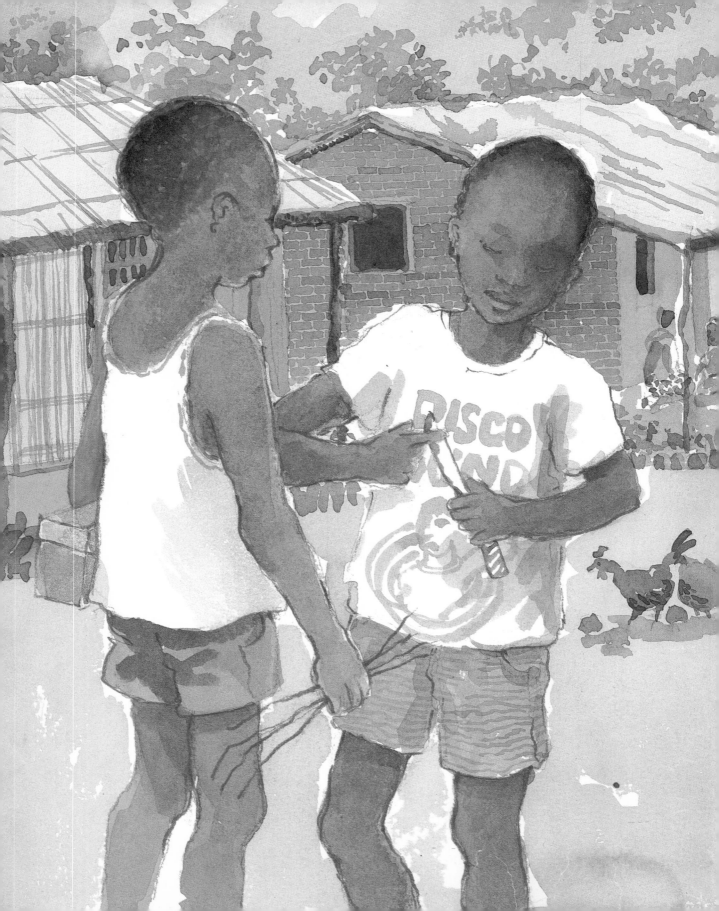

Kondi took his knife and wire scraps and went to the home of his friend, Gift. "I want your wires," Kondi told Gift. "I'll give you my knife for them."

"Why do you want the wires?" Gift asked.

"I want to make a galimoto," Kondi answered.

Gift ran his fingers over the tin knife. "It is a good knife. I'll cut a dancing man with it."

Gift took a handful of wires from his box of things and gave them to Kondi. "That's not enough wire for a galimoto," he told his friend.

"I will find enough wire," Kondi said.

Kondi put his wires into an old white plastic bag and took them to the shop of his uncle. "Good day, second son of my brother," his uncle greeted him. "How can I help you?"

"I want some wire," Kondi told his uncle.

"How will you pay for it?"

"I have no money," Kondi answered, "but you have wires on your old packing boxes from the city. They would make a fine galimoto."

"So you want to make a galimoto. The son of my brother is a clever boy. Take the wires."

Chi, chi, chi, chi. Kondi could hear the grinder at the flour mill. Many women with babies tied on their backs waited in the hot sun. Others arrived carrying heavy baskets of maize on their heads. Kondi squeezed through the crowd.

He was very near the front door when someone grabbed him. The women began yelling angrily. "Stop that one! He goes out of turn." Kondi was being pushed and shoved.

Suddenly the mill stopped its grinding. "What is it?" the miller shouted.

The women pointed at Kondi.

"Ah, no," Kondi said. "I have no maize to grind. I only want wires for a galimoto." He opened his bag for them to see.

"Playthings. For this you keep us waiting," the women grumbled angrily. "One cannot eat wires." An old toothless woman shook her hand at Kondi.

The miller shrugged. "There are some wires out back. Take those and go."

In the back of the mill there was an open door. Inside the door was a pile of old motor parts. There Kondi found some very thin wires wrapped in red and yellow and green plastic. "I can scrape the coating off," Kondi thought. "These wires will hold my galimoto together." Still, he did not have enough for a galimoto.

Kondi passed some young children playing on an anthill. One was Munde, the small sister of his friend, Gift. She had a fine long piece of wire, which she stuck into the hard dirt.

"Little friend," Kondi called as he came nearer, "you cannot catch an ant that way. Go, fetch some water, for with that and a stick we will fool them."

When Munde came back, Kondi poured the water around one of the holes. "Now they will think the rains have begun," he explained. Then he stuck a stick down the hole. Gently he pulled it out, and on the end was a large ant. "My stick is better than a wire for catching ants. You may have the stick, and I'll take the wire."

Kondi knew there was a trash heap behind the bicycle repair shop. But the gate was locked. Kondi climbed over the fence. In the courtyard he found some broken, bent spokes from a bicycle. He climbed back over the fence with his bag.

"Thief! Help! Police! Thief!" Kondi heard a voice call. Children came running from the marketplace. Men came running from the shops. They made a circle around Kondi. "Thief, thief," they chanted, pointing at Kondi.

A policeman arrived. He grabbed Kondi by the shoulder. "What are you doing?" he asked.

Kondi showed the policeman his wires. "I want a galimoto," he explained. "I need these wires."

"Galimoto," the crowd murmured. "Galimoto." They shook their heads and went back to their business.

"Take your wires and go," the policeman told Kondi.

Kondi took his wires back to the shade of the red flame trees in his village. Nearby his mother and sisters pounded their maize. They sang of the hard work they were doing.

Kondi sorted his wires. There were thick pieces and thin pieces. Some wires were long and some were short. Kondi banged the bent and twisted ones with a stone to straighten them.

Then he began. The thick wires made the frame. He wrapped the very thinnest wires at the joints to hold the galimoto together.

"My galimoto will be a pickup," Kondi planned. "It will carry maize to the city. And it will have an antenna for the radio." He smiled.

Kondi worked all afternoon. He pounded the strongest wires around a pipe to make the round wheels. A sturdy piece of bamboo made the rod for the steering wheel.

Finally, the warm toasty smell of maize porridge cooking over the village fires told Kondi it was time to go home. His brothers and sisters admired his work.

"So you found enough wire," Ufulu said.

"Yes," Kondi agreed. He parked his galimoto next to his box of things and ate his supper.

"Let the moon be bright
For us to play and sing tonight."
Kondi could hear his friends singing in the distance. They were calling him to play.

Now he carefully guided his galimoto over the
dusty path. "Galimoto!" someone cheered, and one
by one Kondi's friends formed a line behind him.
"Eeeeeeeeee. Galimoto, Galimoto," they began
to chant.

Kondi saw the shadow of his galimoto, cast by the moonlight, racing alongside.

"It's a fine galimoto," he thought proudly. "Perhaps tomorrow I shall make my galimoto into an ambulance or an airplane or a helicopter."

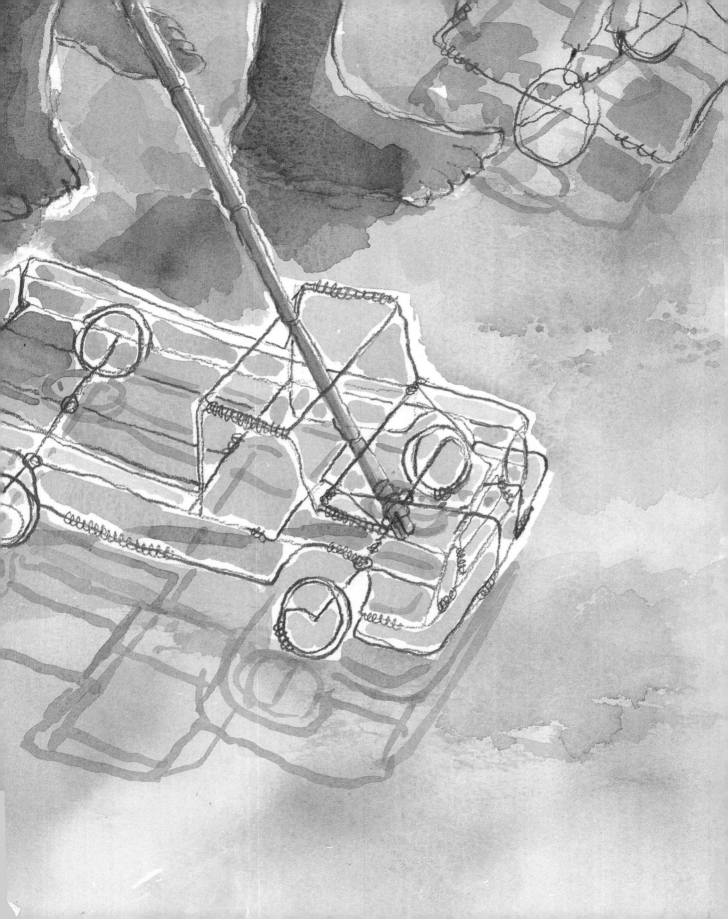